ELMER IN THE SNOW

David McKee

Lothrop, Lee & Shepard Books
New York

One morning, Elmer, the patchwork elephant, met a group of elephants who didn't look very happy.

"What's the matter?" asked Elmer.

"What's the matter is that it's cold," said one of the elephants. "That's what's the matter."

"It's not really cold," said Elmer. "It's just a bit colder than usual. What you need is a good walk to warm you up. Come on, come with me."

For Sabrina B. and Zoë Z.

Reprinted by arrangement with Lothrop, Lee & Shepard, a division of William Morrow and Company, Inc.
Printed in the U.S.A.

Copyright © 1995 by David McKee.
First published in Great Britain by Andersen Press Ltd.

First U.S. Edition   2 3 4 5 6 7 8 9 10
Library of Congress Cataloging in Publication Data was not available in time for the publication of this work,
but it can be obtained from the Library of Congress.
Elmer in the Snow. ISBN 0-688-14596-5. Library of Congress Catalog Card Number 95-77472.

Elmer led the elephants in a direction they didn't normally go. The way went steeply upward, and the elephants were soon puffing with the effort.

"I'm very warm now, thank you, Elmer," said one of the elephants. "Shall we go back now?"

"Not yet," said Elmer. "Keep going."

After they had gone further, an elephant said,
"Elmer, look at the trees. They're different here."
"That's because we are so high up," said Elmer.
"Come on, there's something I want to show you."

A little later, the elephants came out into the open. They stared at the sight—everywhere was white.

"SNOW!" they shouted. Although they had heard about snow, this was the first time they had actually seen any. The elephants roared with laughter as they rushed to play in it.

"It's really cold," called one.

"Cold but fun," laughed another.

"Come look at this," called Elmer. He was
sliding on the ice of a pond that had frozen solid.
One by one the others curiously joined him.

Soon the elephants were slipping and sliding and crashing and falling and really enjoying themselves. They didn't notice Elmer quietly sneak away.

The elephants forgot all about Elmer until they heard his voice nearby.

"Help! Help! I've frozen solid."

The elephants stopped playing and hurried to find Elmer. To their dismay, there stood a white elephant.

"He *has*. He's frozen solid," gasped one of the elephants.

Then he touched the white elephant and a piece
fell off. "It's made of snow!" he said.

"I know where Elmer is," chuckled another.
He pointed to a line of footprints in the snow.
"Come on."

The elephants followed the line of footprints, but before they reached him, Elmer appeared and, with a laugh, started throwing snowballs.

It wasn't long before all the elephants were throwing snowballs at one another.

"It's starting to snow quite hard," said Elmer after a while. "It's time for us to go."

Still laughing and playing, with the snow falling all around them, the elephants hurried back to the trees and then on home.

When they were finally home again, one of the elephants said, "Snow is fun, but it really is cold."

"Yes," said another. "It's nice to be back in the warm."

Elmer said nothing. He just smiled.